AR= 3.4

Fat Bat and Swoop

Fat Bat
and Swoop

LEO LANDRY

An Early Chapter Book

Henry Holt and Company
New York

Henry Holt and Company, LLC
Publishers since 1866
175 Fifth Avenue
New York, New York 10010
www.henryholtchildrensbooks.com

Henry Holt® is a registered trademark of Henry Holt and Company, LLC.
Distributed in Canada by H. B. Fenn and Company Ltd.

Library of Congress Cataloging-in-Publication Data
Landry, Leo.
Fat Bat and Swoop / by Leo Landry.—1st ed.
p.   cm.
Summary: Fat Bat and Swoop the owl play a trick on Emily the cow
but end up getting some of their own medicine.
ISBN-13: 978-0-8050-7003-3
ISBN-10: 0-8050-7003-6
[1. Bats—Fiction. 2. Owls—Fiction. 3. Cows—Fiction.] I. Title.
PZ7.L2317357Fat 2005   [E]—dc22   2005010102

First Edition—2005 / Designed by Patrick Collins
Printed in the United States of America on acid-free paper. ∞

1 3 5 7 9 10 8 6 4 2

*For Terri Schmitz
and The Children's Book Shop*

Contents

Fat Bat and Swoop

→1←

Snacktime

Fat Bat awoke in the dark of night. As usual, his stomach was rumbling.

"Yum!" he said. "Time for bugs!"

So Fat Bat flew off in search of a midnight snack by the light of the summer moon.

As Fat Bat flitted about filling his
belly, his good pal Swoop came along.
Swoop was an owl.

"Hello, Fat Bat," greeted Swoop.
"Finished snacking yet?"

"Never," answered Fat
Bat. "Why do you ask?"

"I am thinking that we could cause a little mischief tonight," offered the owl. "Stir up a little excitement. Bring some life to the dead of night."

"Is that wise?" asked Fat Bat.

"Of course it is," said Swoop. "I am an owl, remember?"

Fat Bat thought about this. "Then let's go," he said.

Fat Bat and Swoop flew off together into the night.

→ 2 ←

Laundry

Fat Bat and Swoop glided over the sleeping farm. As they flapped their wings, they kept their eyes on the ground below.

They saw the pasture where Emily the cow lay sleeping. The neatly trimmed grass shone silver in the moonlight. They saw the Farmers' farmhouse, dark and silent in the night.

They also saw a field mouse chasing a cricket.

"Dinner!" Fat Bat and Swoop shouted.

They dove quickly toward their prey. Fat Bat focused on the cricket. Swoop swooped down on the field mouse.

They did not see the Farmer family's clothesline, neatly hung with freshly washed laundry.

THWOP! went Fat Bat.

THWOP! went Swoop.

Startled by the sound, the field mouse and the cricket quickly dashed to safety. Glancing backward, they saw an eerie sight. The Farmer family's clothes were flying!

A Spooky Idea

"Help!" cried Fat Bat. His batty radar told him that he was now trapped inside of something. "My cricket!" he yelled longingly.

"Help, help!" cried Swoop. His wise owl senses told him that he was definitely in a fix. "Good-bye, delicious mousie!" he hooted sadly.

"Get me out of here!" the pals shouted, struggling with their new wardrobe.

Fat Bat poked his head out of the shirt he was now wearing. "Who put that clothesline there?" he shrieked.

"Those darn Farmers!" cried Swoop. "Always covering their bodies with clothing! They should have been born with something sensible, like feathers!"

"Or at least fur!" said Fat Bat.

"Hmmm . . . wait a minute," said Swoop, popping his head out of the neck of his new sweater. "Look at us. We look like ghosts flying around in the night! I think we could really have some fun spooking someone, since we're dressed like this!"

"You do know who would be fun to surprise, don't you?" Fat Bat asked.

Fat Bat and Swoop looked at each other slyly.

"Emily the cow!" they cried.

→ 4 ←

Ghosts

Fat Bat and Swoop made sure their
new outfits covered them from head to
claw, then flew toward the pasture.
They settled down behind a haystack
and made their plan.

A short distance away, Emily lay
sleeping, dreaming about fields of
sweet green grass.

"We really should let her sleep," said Fat Bat. "She hasn't bothered us lately."

"This will get her back for all of that annoying mooing she does all day long," said Swoop.

"Yes!" agreed Fat Bat. "She always moos while we are trying to sleep!"

"On the count of three, let's both rise up in front of her," whispered Swoop.

"Maybe we should moan," Fat Bat suggested.

"Try using your spookiest voice," said Swoop.

"Emily will think we are ghosts," said Fat Bat. "She is sure to be spooked."

"One . . . two . . . three!" signaled Swoop, waving his wing.

The ghostly pair—one tucked away inside his clean white shirt, the other in his sweater—rose slowly into the moonlight.

→ 5 ←

Boo Whooo

"BOOO!" moaned Fat Bat, flying low over the haystack.

"WHOOO!" hooted his pal Swoop, spreading his wings wide.

"MOOO!" went Emily, waking at once. "MOOOO!"

From behind the haystack, two eerie
white specters rose into the moonlit
night. Emily quickly jumped to her
feet, her eyes bulging in terror. Away
she fled.

Fat Bat and Swoop slowly soared into the sky. They chuckled as they watched Emily the cow dash madly through the farmyard.

"Did you see her run?" asked Fat Bat. "I haven't seen a cow run so fast since we dropped that beehive in the pasture."

"She ran away so fast, the Farmer family is sure to have butter in the morning, instead of fresh milk," joked Swoop. "Well, let's get these clothes back to that clothesline. Whooo, that was fun!"

→ 6 ←

More Laundry

Emily sped through the dark farmyard.
She was so frightened that she did not
watch where she was going.

She didn't see the henhouse and
almost crashed into its side.

She didn't see the tractor and nearly banged her knees against its wheels.

She didn't see the corncrib and almost bumped her chin on its gate.

And she did not see the Farmer
family's clothesline, neatly hung with
freshly washed laundry.

THWOP! went Emily, right into a
large white sheet.

"Mooo!" she cried. "Get me out of here!"

Emily, flailing about in one of the Farmer family's sheets, looked just like a giant ghost.

→ 7 ←

Scared Friends

Fat Bat and Swoop were still laughing as they turned the corner of the farm-house. "I'll never forget the look on her face," said Swoop, chuckling.

"We've really topped ourselves this time," giggled Fat Bat. "She really thought we were—"

"MOOOO!" moaned Emily as she wrestled with the sheet. She was so tangled up, she couldn't see where she was going.

Fat Bat and Swoop stopped in mid-flight. They saw a large white object straight ahead, flailing about spookily. It was making a terrible noise—and coming right toward them!

Fat Bat gulped and Swoop's eyes bulged in terror.

"GHOST!" they shrieked together, and they zipped away as fast as their wings would carry them.

→ 8 ←

Hmmm . . .

Wings shaking, Fat Bat and Swoop met back at the tree. "Did you see that?" gasped Fat Bat.

"That was a real ghost," answered Swoop, his voice quavering. "I am sure of it."

"It had to be a ghost." Fat Bat was trembling. "Did you see the way its hooves were flailing about, trying to scare us?"

Swoop thought hard for a moment, shifting from one talon to the other. Soon his curiosity overcame his fear.

"Fat Bat, did you say 'hooves'?" asked Swoop. "Hmmm . . . I wonder." He shifted on his talons again. "Fat Bat, let's make a quick flight back to that clothesline," he said. "Maybe it wasn't a ghost after all."

"I'm not going back there," said Fat Bat. "Now we've woken a real ghost! I knew we should have let Emily sleep!" He hung upside down, wings wrapped around himself in fear, eyes closed.

"Fat Bat," said Swoop, "I think the ghost was Emily."

"You . . . you do?" exclaimed Fat Bat. He opened one eye to peek at his friend. "But how . . ."

"Just come with me," said Swoop confidently.

⇥ **9** ⇤

Confessions

Fat Bat and Swoop returned to the Farmer family's clothesline.

There was Emily, untangling herself from a large white sheet.

Fat Bat and Swoop put two and two together. Emily *had* been their ghost.

She looked up warily as the pair flew closer.

"Hello, Fat Bat. Hello, Swoop," she grumbled.

"Er . . . hello, Emily," said Fat Bat nervously.

"What are you doing up at this hour?" Swoop asked.

"Someone seems to have played a prank on me," she answered. "Again." She sighed. "Though I don't know why. I've never bothered anyone on the farm."

"Of course not," said Swoop.

Fat Bat and Swoop looked at each other. They felt guilty.

"Well, there is that constant mooing all day long," said Fat Bat.

"That may be annoying to the nighttime animals on the farm, who are trying to get a good day's sleep," Swoop added.

Emily looked at Fat Bat and Swoop suspiciously, wondering if they were trying to tell her something.

"I'm only mooing like that because I'm lonely," she replied. "It's not easy being the only cow on the farm, you know. Nobody thinks that I'd like to join in any of the fun around here."

"We're sorry for scaring you," said Fat Bat.

"It was you!" cried Emily.

"We only meant to have a little fun," said Swoop. "And we never thought you would like hanging around with a couple of nocturnal creatures, so we've never asked."

"All right," Emily said, "apology accepted." She brightened. "I suppose you nighttime animals aren't so bad after all."

→ 10 ←
Three Friends

Fat Bat and Swoop huddled together, their wings around each other's shoulders, whispering.

"What are you two up to now?" asked Emily.

"If it makes you feel any better," explained Fat Bat, "when you were all tangled up in that sheet, Swoop and I thought you were a ghost. We flew for our lives!"

"Now that's funny!" answered Emily. "That makes waking up in the middle of the night worthwhile!"

Fat Bat and Swoop exchanged
glances.

"Say, Emily," asked Swoop, "would
you like to join us for a little mischief
at the henhouse?"

Emily thought for a moment. Then a little grin appeared on her face. "Do you really think that's wise?" she asked.

"Of course it is," said Swoop. "I am an owl, remember?"

"Then let's go," decided Emily.

And Fat Bat, Swoop, and their new friend, Emily, headed off together into the night.